I come from a big family, and I missed my brothers and sisters, Angie, Bill, Flossie, Beppo, Moll, Chrysanthemum and Sid. My real name is Boojer, not Terry, but nobody knew that any more.

"I'm sick of this," I said. "I want to get out and find another rabbit to talk to."

YOUNG CORGI BOOKS

Young Corgi books are perfect when you are looking for great books to read on your own. They are full of exciting stories and entertaining pictures. There are funny books, scary books, spine-tingling stories and mysterious ones. Whatever your interests you'll find something in Young Corgi to suit you: from ponies to football, from families to ghosts. The books are written by some of the most famous and popular of today's children's authors, and by some of the best new talents, too.

Whether you read one chapter a night, or devour the whole book in one sitting, you'll love Young Corgi books. The more you read, the more you'll want to read!

Other Young Corgi books to get your teeth into
BUMBLE by Alison Prince
LIZZIE ZIPMOUTH
by Jacqueline Wilson
ANIMAL CRACKERS
by Narinder Dhami

Also available in Corgi Pups
CAT NUMBER 3 by Alison Prince

BOOJER

To Lindsey and the couple in the kitchen

BOOJER
A YOUNG CORGI BOOK : 0 552 547875

PRINTING HISTORY
Young Corgi edition published 2002

1 3 5 7 9 10 8 6 4 2

Set in 17/21pt Bembo Schoolbook by
Phoenix Typesetting, Ilkley, West Yorkshire

Young Corgi Books are published by Transworld Publishers,
61–63 Uxbridge Road, London W5 5SA,
a division of The Random House Group Ltd,
in Australia by Random House Australia (Pty) Ltd,
20 Alfred Street, Milsons Point, Sydney, NSW 2061, Australia,
in New Zealand by Random House New Zealand Ltd,
18 Poland Road, Glenfield, Auckland 10, New Zealand
and in South Africa by Random House (Pty) Ltd,
Endulini, 5a Jubilee Road, Parktown 2193, South Africa

Printed and bound in Great Britain by
Cox & Wyman Ltd, Reading, Berkshire

Booter

ALISON PRINCE

Illustrated by Kate Sheppard

YOUNG CORGI

Chapter One

I was shut up in a small hutch with nobody to talk to, and I was bored. Badly, horribly, seriously bored. Apart from the mice who came out at night, nobody said a word to me from one week to the next. And it was driving me up the wall.

I belonged to a boy called Eggy.
His real name was Egbert – at least,
that's what his mother shouted at him
when she was cross. He was boring,
too. He never did anything, just sat in
a room where a blue light flickered –
I could see it through the window.

Once night I asked
the mice about the
blue light, and
Kevin said, "Telly,
innit." He and his
friends were in and
out of houses all
the time, so they
knew about things
like that, but I didn't.

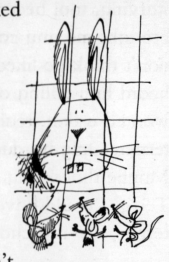

Marlene explained. "It's like
moving pictures," she said. "Only
they're not real. You can't smell
them or touch them or eat them,
they're just for looking at. Stupid,
really, but that's humans for you."
Then she added, "Talking of eating
things, I'm starving. Anyone coming
on a kitchen raid?"

"Yeah, cool," the others said, and
off they went.

All right for some, I thought. I was

starving, too, because Eggy hadn't brought me any carrots or hay. I don't think he liked rabbits much. I heard him telling a friend he'd wanted a dog, really. A Jack Russell terrier. Only his dad wouldn't have it. Maybe that's why he called me Terry. I could have been a good terrier, given a chance.

Terry the terrier. I'd have gone for walks and dug holes and chewed things up, the way terriers do. I couldn't have barked, though – rabbits don't. Pity, really. Eggy might have brought me something to eat if he'd heard me barking in my hutch. As it was, he just went on forgetting.

I got more and more fed up. I come from a big family, and I missed my brothers and sisters, Angie, Bill, Flossie, Beppo, Moll, Chrysanthemum and Sid. My real name is Boojer, not Terry, but nobody knew that any more.

"I'm sick of this," I told the mice. "I want to get out and find another rabbit to talk to."

"No probs," said Kevin. "We'll have your door open in a jiff. Come on, lads."

He and Darren
and a few others
tugged at the bolt
on my hutch door,
and Marlene and
Janice joined in as
well, but it was too
heavy for them.
"Sorry, mate,"
Kevin told me. "Can't shift it. You'll
have to find some other way." Then
they all trooped off to wreck another
kitchen.

I tried to escape whenever Eggy
brought me some food, but it was no
good – he just bundled me back in

again. He got a bit
scratched one
day. I didn't do
it on purpose,
I was only
scrabbling to
try and get
out, but he
went off sucking
his hand and grum-
bling, and after that he forgot more
often than ever to feed me.

I started biting at the wood in the
corner of my hutch. It didn't taste
very nice, but my teeth were growing
long, and I needed
something to
chew. Then one
night I suddenly
found I'd bitten
a hole right
through the wall.

My nose and whiskers were out in
the fresh air that smelt of grass and
dandelions, and when I pushed a bit
more, I got my whole head out. It
was wonderful – I could see the stars
in the sky.

The mice came to look. "Hey,
Terry's getting out!" said Marlene.
"Fantastic!"

I did a lot more biting, and scrabbled with my claws. Chips of wood flew everywhere, and the hole got bigger.

"Come on!" shouted the mice. "You can do it!"

I pushed my head and front paws through, then nearly got stuck – but with one more heave, I was out and rolling in the grass while the mice clapped and cheered.

"T'riffic," said Kevin. "Now you can come kitchen-raiding with us." But Marlene shook her head and said, "We'd never get him through our tunnels."

"She's right," said Darren. "Pity, though. Would have been great, taking a rabbit along – look at the size of him. Like a bulldozer."

I had more to do than run around with a gang of mice. They were very nice in their way, but I wanted another rabbit to talk to. So I said, "Thanks for the thought, but I'm going to be busy."

They didn't mind. "OK," they said. "See you around." And I made for the gate.

Chapter Two

Outside, there was no grass or earth, just flat pavement and then the road, hard and black. No good for rabbits. I thought it might be better on the other side, but I'd just started to cross

when – WHOOSH! – a huge thing, much bigger than Eggy's dad's car, went roaring past. It made a noise like a thunderstorm, and the ground shook.

I turned back from that dangerous place and ran off along the pavement, past the hedges and fences and closed gates of other houses. I didn't know where I was going, but it wasn't back

to Eggy, that was for sure. I shot past
a man, and he was so surprised that
he nearly fell over. "A rabbit?" he
said. "Am I seeing things?"

Such a stupid question. He was
seeing the pavement, wasn't he, and
the hedge and the road and me? But
as Marlene might have said, that's
humans for you. I galloped on –
then at last I came to an open gate,
and dived through it.

Inside, there was a quiet, wonderfully weedy garden. Nobody had cut the grass for weeks, and it was full of tasty dandelions and daisies. Flowers blossomed untidily and bushes

sprawled about, with good hidey-places underneath them. A light shone from one of the windows of the house, but it wasn't the flickering blue sort.

Music was playing, and sometimes a man sang along with it. I hopped about, nibbling here and there, and it was all very nice. If there had been another rabbit around, it would have been even nicer, but even so, it was a lot better than the hutch. When I'd eaten enough, I dug out a little hollow among the dry leaves under a bush, and went to sleep.

I slept late the next morning – and when I woke, I nearly died of fright. Three cats were staring at me. Two of them were ginger and the third was small and black.

"Rabbit," said the black one, and licked her lips.

It was a very nasty moment. She wasn't as big as me, but there was something about the way she smiled that made me feel quite faint.

"Jezebel, don't be so horrid," one of the gingers scolded. "He's a visitor. You can't eat visitors."

"I don't see why not," said Jezebel. The gingers looked at each other and sighed. "She's dreadful," said the one who had spoken. Then he turned to me and added, "I'm Bert, by the way, and this is Whistle. Who are you?"

"Eggy called me Terry," I said. "My real name's Boojer."

"Who's Eggy?" asked Bert.

"I used to live in his hutch, but I escaped."

"Why?" asked Whistle.

"He was boring." I didn't want to mention the lack of food in case it made Jezebel feel more hungry.

"I'm never bored," said Bert. "Are you, Whistle?"

"No," said Whistle. "There's such interesting things to do. Like – um – sleeping."

"And eating," said Jezebel. She was still looking at me as if I was a tasty dinner. "Are you going to live here?" she added. "I do hope so."

"No, thanks," I said rather quickly. "Just passing through."

"Pity," said Jezebel.

At that moment a man opened the back door and called, "Breakfast!" and the black cat streaked across the grass to twine herself round his legs.

"Dreadful," the gingers sighed together. Then they got up and followed her, though much more slowly. One of them turned to say, "See you later" – but I was already on my way towards the neighbouring hedge.

Chapter Three

The garden next door had no cats in it, but there was nothing much else, either. No grass, no nice weeds, just paving stones and deckchairs and a kind of outdoor cooking thing that smelt alarmingly of sausages. I couldn't find a way out, so I started to burrow under their ornamental wall, wanting to get through to the garden on the other side.

A woman shrieked from the window, "Rodney, there's a rabbit digging up the patio!"

I dug faster, and Rodney came out in his dressing gown with a cup of coffee in one hand and a newspaper in the other. He flapped the

paper at me and shouted, "Shoo!"
and at that moment, I broke through
into the garden next door and left
Rodney behind.

He went shuffling back to the
house in his slippers. "That fixed
him," he said. And the woman said,
"Rodney, you're wonderful."

The garden I found myself in wasn't much good, either. It had paths made of stone chips, with a pond in the middle where little plastic humans in red jackets sat round, holding fishing rods. There  were no fish in the pond, but they weren't going to catch anything anyway, being plastic. I moved on.

Next door, there was a jungle of long grass and old prams and bits of motor cars. I quite liked it in there. It had a good selection of weeds and nice places where brambles grew – but then a huge dog came bounding

out, with a man behind him shouting,
"Rabbit stew, rabbit stew! Get him,
Rocky!" So I dived through a gap in
the fence, and left the dog barking
behind me.

On the other side, nothing grew at
all except parked cars, and boys were
whizzing about between them on little
boards with wheels.

"Hey, look, there's a rabbit!" one of them shouted. He came rushing towards me, so I shot under a car and out the other side, but there were more boys on wheels there and they all came zooming after me. I never knew I could run so fast. Round and round

we went, in and out between cars with me darting underneath them and the boys swooping and shouting – and then they had me cornered by a rubbish bin. Boys all round me, no way out. My heart was thumping with fear.

One of the boys slid forward and picked me up. "What'll we do with him?" he asked.

"Perhaps he's hungry," said another one. "Tell you what! Let's put him in old Meanie's garden."

"He'll go mad," said the first boy. "Who, the rabbit?"

"No, Meanie. You know what he's like. Remember when our football landed in his cabbages?"

The other boy laughed and said, "Carried on like a maniac, didn't he? Come on, then – this should be a laugh."

They carried me past all the cars and put me carefully over the wall. And on the other side was rabbit heaven.

Rows and rows of delicious veget-
ables were growing in straight, tidy
lines. There were carrots with
feathery, sweet-smelling tops, succulent
peas hanging among their green
leaves, plump cabbages, tasty celery,
cauliflowers almost bigger than I was,
and lettuces of every shape and kind. I
couldn't believe my eyes.

I lolloped along the rows, taking a bite out of everything. I dug the earth away from carrots and sugary-tasting parsnips and peppery turnips, and tried every one of all the different lettuces. It was wonderful. All I needed was a rabbit friend to share it with, and I'd have been in paradise.

Then I saw the man.

He was standing beside his tomato plants (I'd tasted those as well) holding a hoe, and his face was purple.

"AAAAARGH!" he bellowed. "MY LETTUCES!" Then he said a whole lot of words I'd never heard before, very loudly, and shook the hoe in the air. The boys were looking over the wall, grinning. I tried to

creep away under the shelter of some beetroot leaves, but the hoe-man saw me.

"COME HERE!" he yelled.

I didn't, of course – I'm not stupid. I turned and fled. The man chased me down the bean rows and round the

courgette clumps and over the compost heap and past the green-house, through the beetroot and the

kale, the chives and chicory and radishes, and in desperation I headed along the path that ran past his house,

out through the front gate and across
the pavement to the road and—

EEE-EEE-EEEK!

A car skidded to a stop with its
front wheel almost touching me,

and it jumped even closer as the one
behind bumped into it. There was a

lot of hooting and shouting, and the man in the nearest car yelled at the man with the hoe, "WHY DON'T YOU CONTROL YOUR BLASTED RABBIT?"

"*IT'S NOT MY RABBIT!*" the hoe-man yelled back. "*I HATE RABBITS!*"

I sat in the road with my eyes shut and my ears pressed against my back, too terrified to move.

Chapter Four

Somebody lifted me up. A girl with glasses and a fringe of brown hair.

"Oh, he's *sweet*!" she said. "Look at his little black nose. And he's so scared."

"I'll give him scared," said the hoe-man. "If he comes in my garden again, he'll have nibbled his last lettuce, I'll tell you that."

"Well, he won't," said the girl, hugging me more tightly. "Because I'm going to look after him. I'll take him to school."

"Fine time to be going to school," the man said. "Half past blooming eleven. Kids these days – I don't know."

"I've been to the dentist, that's all," the girl said. "And just as well, or I wouldn't have been here." She stroked my ears. "Poor little thing."

"Huh!" said the man. "Poor little thing be blowed." And he went grumbling off to his tomatoes. "You'll be a friend for Bingo," the girl told me as we went along. "He'll like that – I'm sure he's been lonely."

My ears pricked up at the thought. Did she mean she had a rabbit already? That would be great. Bingo wouldn't be as good as Angie, Bill, Flossie, Beppo, Moll, Chrysanthemum and Sid, but he'd be a lot better than nothing. We'd have some very enjoyable fights, sorting out which of us was top rabbit.

The girl took me over the road and in through big gates to a building that was full of children rushing about and talking. "Don't be scared," she said, "it's only a school." But it was very noisy, so I shut my eyes again. When I opened them, we were in a room with big windows. There were a lot of children in here, too, and they all came crowding round to look at me and stroke me.

"Rosie, *really*," said the lady in charge of them. "This is a school, not a farm. Why have you brought a rabbit?"

"It wasn't my fault, Mrs Burton, honestly it wasn't," Rosie said. "He was in someone's garden and a man was chasing him and he nearly got run over."

Mrs Burton sighed. "Well, put him in with the guinea pigs for now," she said, "and we'll try to find out where he's come from. Nobody here has lost a rabbit, have they? White, with a black nose? Quite unusual."

The children shook their heads. One of them looked bigger and rounder than the others, and suddenly I knew who he was.

Eggy.

I froze with horror. My escape had been for nothing. Eggy would say I was his, and I'd be back in that hutch with nobody to talk to but the mice.

Eggy glanced at me, and his ears turned rather red – but he didn't say a word, just stared down at the table and scowled. I couldn't believe it. He knew who I was all right, but he wasn't saying. Perhaps he thought if I didn't come back, he might get a dog instead.

Rosie carried me over to a big cage that stood on a table and put me in. The two guinea pigs who lived there said, "EEEEK!" and disappeared into their bedroom.

I kept very still, and after a bit they peeped out.

"What is it?" one of them whispered to the other.

"I don't know," she whispered back. "It's big, isn't it?"

"And scary."

"A big, scary thing," they both said. "EEEEK!" And they'd gone again.

I stayed where I was. Next time they looked out, I said, "I'm not a scary thing, I'm a rabbit."

The guinea pigs thought about this very carefully, then one of them asked, "How do you know?"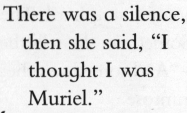

"I just am," I said. "Like you're guinea pigs."

There was a silence, then she said, "I thought I was Muriel."

"And I'm Primrose," agreed the other one.

I was beginning to see why rabbits think guinea pigs are a bit dim. "And this is a school," I said, trying to be helpful. "Rosie told me."

"Um – yes." They didn't seem quite sure. I'd heard Eggy and his friends talk about school sometimes when they came to his house to watch the blue light, but I'd never known what it was.

"What do they do here?" I asked. "I mean, why do the children come here? What's it for?"

The guinea pigs gazed at me blankly, then gazed at each other.

"What's it for?" murmured Primrose.

They both scratched their heads and thought very hard. Then Muriel said, "Sometimes she tells them to sit down."

"And sometimes they do," said Primrose.

After that, exhausted by so much thinking, they tottered into their bedroom and went to sleep.

Chapter Five

I went to sleep as well – it had been a busy morning. When I woke up, the children were putting their chairs on the tables. Rosie lifted me out of the cage, but Mrs Burton said, "I think you should ask your mum before you take him home."

At that moment, a woman came into the room, carrying a basket with a wire-mesh front.

"Hello, Mrs Cats-Home!" said Rosie, beaming.

Mrs Burton looked shocked. "I'm sure that's not this lady's name," she said.

"Critchley-Hetherington, actually," said the basket woman, "but nobody can manage it. About this rabbit."

"How did you know I'd found him?" asked Rosie. She was still smiling.

"Someone phoned me to say theirs was missing," Mrs Cats-Home said, "and then I heard that a girl had rescued an escaped rabbit from the road. Glasses – brown hair – I thought it must be you." She glanced round and spotted Eggy, who was trying to slide out of the door. "Egbert – it was your mum who phoned."

"Was it?" said Eggy.

Everyone stared at him, and Rosie looked puzzled. "Why didn't you say you'd lost your rabbit?" she asked.

"Didn't know," said Eggy.

Rosie frowned. "But you must have known. Was he in his hutch this morning?"

Eggy shrugged and said, "Dunno." His ears were very red now, and so was his face.

"But didn't you go out to feed him?" Rosie asked.

"Forgot," said Eggy.

Mrs Cats-Home said, "I think I'm rather sorry for your rabbit."

"He scratched me," said Eggy. "My dad says he's vicious."

"No, he's not!" Rosie protested. I thought she meant Eggy's dad, but she went on, "Just look at his little black nose. He's sweet."

Eggy looked, but he didn't seem to think I was sweet.

"Well, if you don't want him, can I have him?" asked Rosie.

"S'pose so, yeah," said Eggy.

And Rosie beamed and said, "Oh, good."

"But your mother—" began Mrs Burton.

"She won't mind," said Rosie. "She never does. And Dad will just shut his eyes and hold his head. He's getting used to animals now we've got a cat and a dog and a rabbit as well as a hamster."

Mrs Cats-Home was undoing the basket. "Pop him in here, Rosie," she said, "it's safer than carrying him."

Rosie put me in and did up the wire mesh, and I heard a murmur from the guinea pigs' cage.

"He's gone, Primrose."

"Who has?"

"The scary thing."

"Was there a scary thing?"

"I don't know. Perhaps I dreamt it."

"Perhaps you did."

Gentle snores began again. Those two were never bored, I thought, because everything was such a puzzle to them.

Rosie carried my basket along the roads, and Mrs Cats-Home came, too. We went into a house.

"Oh, Rosie," said her mother. "What now?"

"Just another rabbit, that's all," said Rosie. "A friend for Bingo. I've rescued him from Eggy and from a man who grows lettuces and from being run over. His name's Terry. Eggy said."

"Oh, well, I suppose . . ." said her mother.

"Don't put him straight into Bingo's hutch, or they'll probably fight," Mrs Cats-Home warned. "Boy rabbits always do."

"Bingo's out in his run," said Rosie's mum. "Let's see if they get on all right. If they don't, Terry will have to go."

They carried me outside, and Rosie lowered me carefully into the big, wire run . . .

And there was Bingo. Beautiful
Bingo, who wasn't a boy at all. She
was the girl of every rabbit's dreams,
and she stared at me as if she
couldn't believe her eyes. Then we
both ran mad circles because we
were so excited, and touched noses
with our whiskers bristling.

"There," said Rosie. "You can see they really like each other. Sweet. So Terry can stay, can't he?"

"I must be off," said Mrs Cats-Home, doing up the basket. "I have to go and fetch five kittens. Would you like one?"

"Oh, Mum, couldn't we—?"

"*No*," said Rosie's mum.

Things are fine now. Bingo and I have a lovely family: Peppi, Petunia, Slocum, Dolores, Bruno, Christopher and Bud. Bingo calls me Boojer, of course, but Rosie doesn't know that.

And I'm never bored for a minute.

THE END